PICTURE GIRL

Picture Girl

Marlene Targ Brill

Golden Alley Press
Emmaus, Pennsylvania

Golden Alley Press
37 S. Sixth Street
Emmaus, PA 18049

www.goldenalleypress.com

The text of this book is set in ITC Usherwood
Book designed by Michael Sayre

Printed in United States of America

Publisher's Cataloging-in-Publication Data

Names: Brill, Marlene Targ, author. | Sayre, Michael, 1957- illustrator.
Title: Picture girl / Marlene Targ Brill ; [illustrated by] Michael Sayre.
Description: Emmaus, PA : Golden Alley Press, 2018. | Series: Becoming American kids, bk. 1. | Summary: In 1922, Luba and her family must flee the Ukraine in hopes of finding sanctuary in America. | Grades 3-6.
Identifiers: LCCN 2018946750 | ISBN 978-1-7320276-0-2 (pbk.) | ISBN 978-1-7320276-1-9 (ebook)
Subjects: LCSH: Pogroms–Ukraine–Juvenile fiction. | CYAC: Jews–Ukraine–Fiction. | Immigrants–United States–Fiction. | Ellis Island (N.J. and N.Y.)–History–Fiction. | New York (N.Y.)–Fiction. | Historical fiction. | BISAC: JUVENILE FICTION / Historical / General. | JUVENILE FICTION / Social Themes / Emigration & Immigration. | JUVENILE FICTION / Social Themes / Prejudice & Racism.
Classification: LCC PZ7.7.B75 Pic 2018 (print) | LCC PZ7.7.B75 (ebook) | DDC [Fic]–dc23.

10 9 8 7 6 5 4 3 2 1

For Louise,
who kindly shared her story with me,
and for all the young artists
who change lives with
their pictures

ZHITOMIR
UKRAINE

ZHITOMIR, UKRAINE

1922

The Characters:

Solomon Dichne, Papa

Genia Dichne, Mama

Luba, age 12

Moysey, age 11

Fayvish, age 10

Yankel and Sonia, 5-year-old twins

Danger in Zhitomir

Luba gasped as she opened the red front door of her house. The kitchen and dining room looked like a tornado had blown through them. Some cabinets were bare. Rumpled clothes oozed out of dresser drawers. More clothing and blankets lay piled on the floors.

The strangest sight of all was seeing Papa home from his leather shop. He never returned from work before dinner time. Often, he stayed until after sundown. Now Papa held a crying Mama in his arms. Seeing Luba, Mama pushed away from Papa.

"What happened, Mama?" Luba asked. "Why is Papa home? Why are you crying, Mama?"

"Hush, Luba. We must leave quickly," Mama ordered, wiping her tears. "Put on another layer of clothes."

"Where are we going, Mama?" Luba asked louder. "Please tell me what happened."

"No more questions now," Mama said. "Once you dress, please help your little sister. After she's dressed, make sure your brothers are wearing extra layers of clothes in case they need warmth or must change something. We'll talk once we're ready to leave."

Luba noticed that Papa frowned, a sign that he was worried. Mama dabbed away more tears with her handkerchief. They both raced from room to room, shoving articles into bags—some to hide and some to take with them. They closed all the window shutters. Papa stowed jewelry and candlesticks under the secret floorboard. He tucked silver holiday plates in the back of the closet under tablecloths. Mama grabbed blankets and pillows and threw them in a pile. She stuffed bread, cheese, and jam into a sack.

Luba left to find Moysey, Fayvish, and Yankel, her younger brothers, hiding in their room.

"Do you know what's happening?" Luba asked them. Moysey shook his head no. Fayvish shrugged his shoulders. Little Yankel ran to Luba and buried his head in her skirt.

"Well, we must do as Mama says," Luba said, taking Yankel's head in her hands and giving him a kiss. The boys were used to Luba ordering them around, she being the oldest and originator of most of their games. They looked up to her to guide them.

Luba called for five-year-old Sonia, Yankel's twin sister, to join them in the boy's room. "Bring your two favorite sweaters and skirts with you," Luba told Sonia. "You boys put on another layer of pants and sweaters." Everyone, including Luba, dressed quickly.

"We're about ready," Luba called to her parents once everyone was almost dressed. "What should we do now?"

"Come here," Papa called.

Luba pushed the children down the hall and into the darkened dining room. Mama pointed to places for them to sit. Luba gave Sonia's favorite pink sweater one last tug to smooth it over her blue sweater and blouse. Then she lifted Sonia onto her lap.

Mama wiped her hands on her apron. "Come close, my little ones," she said, opening her arms wide. After hugging each child, she gave them orders.

"Fayvish and Moysey, pack a small bag of books and toys to keep you busy and out of trouble," Mama said to Luba's 10- and 11-year-old brothers. "Luba, help Yankel and Sonia do the same, and you bring some treasures to keep you busy, too. We must hide in the Warshaver's cellar. We have no idea how long we must stay there.

"After you each fill your special bag, Luba will take the twins' hands and follow us," Mama said, motioning toward Yankel and Sonia. "Boys, you will follow Luba. And no more questions. We must be very quiet. Papa heard that the Cossacks are coming again. This time, they are killing everyone in their path. We must head to our neighbors' cellar—and quickly. The sun is setting."

A chill ran through Luba's body. She

remembered how the cruel soldiers who served the Russian government had charged through town on horseback a few months ago. These horrible giants in big hats and long black coats cut the air with their swords. And the hate in their eyes for Jewish families! They had been attacking Jewish communities all over Ukraine. They blamed Jews for the bad harvest that caused peasants to starve and falsely accused them of being traitors during the terrible Great War that had just ended.

Luba glanced up at the pictures hanging on the wall, pictures that she had drawn and painted. Would they still be hanging there when she returned? No matter, she thought, shaking herself back to the present. My family must stay safe first.

"Do as Mama says and come, Yankel," Luba said, holding out a hand to her brother. For once, the five-year-old did as he was told.

"You, too, Sonia," she said. Sonia squeezed her big sister's other hand.

The children hurried to their rooms to choose what to bring with them. Yankel stood still, looking around. "Quickly," Luba said. After a minute that seemed like hours, he chose a small wooden wagon that Luba had helped him build and marbles to put into it. For Sonia, it was easy. She had a special doll she loved more than anything. And she liked to string beads.

Luba wanted no other choice than her colored pencils and notebook. Drawing was her favorite thing to do. Each day after school she drew pictures, sometimes with her art teacher Mikhail. Tonight, she hoped drawing would take her mind off the scary soldiers.

Once the twins and Luba finished packing, they tiptoed into the dark yard after their parents, who carried piles of food and bedding. Brothers Fayvish and Moysey followed. Each held a bag with books, paper, pencils and small toys.

The Dichne family crossed into their neighbors' yard. After pulling open a flat wooden door next to the house, they felt their way down a dark staircase into the cellar. Fayvish and Moysey clung to each other to keep from tripping. The Warshavers were waiting for them in the cellar.

Once the entire Dichne family was downstairs, Mr. Warshaver bolted the door from the inside. He lit a candle. "Help your friend Moysey with his bags," Mr. Warshaver told his son Izia.

Mrs. Warshaver and Mama spread blankets on the floor. "Rest, my children," Mama said. "This will be our home for the night."

PICTURE GIRL

2

The Long Wait

Luba covered Sonia and Yankel with their blankets. Once the twins were settled, she slipped under her own blanket. But she couldn't sleep. The cellar felt damp and cool. Her body shivered from fear as much as cold. She kept wondering what would happen to them.

Hate-filled Cossacks stormed their little village whenever they pleased. The Russian government, who hired these monsters to stop peasant uprisings, never stopped the soldiers-for-hire. The first time they came, the soldiers had wrecked Papa's shop. They smashed the store window and scattered

Papa's tools that once sat neatly on their shelves. But Papa never complained. He fixed the broken store window. He arranged his leather tools back on the shelves. "At least my family is alive," he had said. "Other shopkeepers were not so lucky."

Luba remembered another visit from the angry Cossacks, this time while Papa was away at work. Mama and the children had hidden in the Warshaver's cellar with other women and children from the village. But the Cossacks had discovered them hiding there. The soldiers shouted at them to open the cellar door. If they refused, they said, they would set the house on fire with everyone in it.

When the women did as they were told, the Cossacks demanded their money and jewelry. Luba and her brothers and sister clung to Mama, trembling as the Cossacks went from one woman to another. When the men came to Mama, she stood still as stone.

"Give me your jewelry," one man growled.

Mama stood frozen in place. The Cossack raised his sword. Fearing for her mother's life, Luba pulled Mama's wedding ring off her finger. Then the eleven-year-old took money from

Mama's pocket. Luba handed everything to the soldiers. Otherwise, they were ready to beat Mama—or worse.

Luba never wanted to worry about Mama's life again. She never wanted to take anything from Mama again. She was glad that Mama and Papa hid their priceless belongings this time.

For days, Luba's family and the Warshavers ate and slept in the same candle-lit, damp cellar. Space was small and nerves were jumpy. At least Luba had paper and pencils to help calm her. But the children eventually tired of drawing and reading by candlelight. With nothing else to do, they teased each other. They picked fights.

"Stop yelling," their parents insisted. "No fighting. And be quiet." Everyone was grumpier than usual.

After their children were asleep, the adults talked about what was happening. They huddled together and whispered about what to do. Mostly they complained and worried. They wondered what the soldiers were doing to their community.

"I'll check what has happened to our village," Papa said on the morning of the sixth day. "We cannot stay cooped up like animals. The children need fresh air to breathe. They need to run."

"It's too dangerous," Mama said. She held his arm.

"No, we need to see if we can leave. I will be safe," Papa insisted. "Besides, people never think I am Jewish with my blue eyes and blond hair, like Luba's. Wait for me to give you a sign that we can return home."

Papa pulled away from Mama. He climbed the stairs and opened the cellar door. Light shone on the stairs for the first time in almost a week.

Mama sank into the corner crying. The twins joined her, creating a chorus of weepy sounds. Luba took out another piece of paper to draw.

Papa seemed to be gone for hours. After a while Luba heard tapping on the cellar door.

"Mama, children, come out!" Papa called. "We are free now."

Mama opened the cellar door and ran to hug him. Luba started collecting their blankets, clothes, and other belongings.

"Moysey, Fayvish, carry your own blankets and books," Luba ordered. "You, too, Sonia and Yankel."

"Stop being so bossy," Moysey said. Still he gathered his dirty clothes and games.

Papa thanked the Warshavers. Then Mama and Papa led the ragtag group across the yards to their home. Luba followed her brothers and sister. "Your blanket is dragging, Fayvish. You dropped your doll, Sonia," Luba said.

Upon entering the house Mama let out a little scream, this time for joy. "We were spared. Our home remains in order," she said.

"The Cossacks mostly damaged around the market square and the synagogues," Papa said. "Now let's eat, take a bath, and sleep in our own beds."

That night, Mama and Papa tucked each child into bed. Luba pretended to be asleep, but she still worried what would happen to them. They were safe for now, but what about the next time the soldiers came?

She strained to hear her parents talking in the kitchen. Papa told Mama what he had seen in the village while they hid in the cellar.

"Raiders burned out stores and homes on the other side of town. My leather shop is wrecked.

The Cossacks stole my tools. I can no longer work there," Papa said. "Between litter from damage and bodies in the street, the sights tore at my heart. We need to think about a future beyond our beloved town of Zhitomir."

Tears rolled down Luba's cheek. Her happy life was changing—and fast. After each raid, the village tried to return to everyday chores. But the raids were coming more often now. This time, her family could no longer pretend that they could restart their usual life. At least she could escape at school until her parents decided what to do.

3

Trouble at School

Luba went to a school run by the Eastern Orthodox Church. Her parents felt it was the best place for an education. The school rarely took Jewish girls. But Luba scored so high on exams that she was one of the few Jews let into the school.

Luba proudly wore the school's uniform. A white apron covered her brown dress. Every Sunday, school rules forced her to go to church services. A priest sprinkled the girls with holy water, which Jews do not do. Luba never questioned what happened at school. She never told her parents. She was at school to improve her arithmetic, geography, Russian, French, and German. She cared little about the religion taught at school. In fact, she liked that she learned one religion at school and lived another with her family.

Even though there were many Jews living in Zhitomir, neither the public school where the boys went, nor the church school Luba attended allowed for Hebrew education. Papa was a modern thinker who insisted that all his children, even the girls, learn how to read and write Hebrew.

Not every Jewish family felt the same way. Girls usually learned prayers for lighting Friday night candles and for blessings over wine and certain foods. But they were not allowed to read from the Bible. Papa did not agree with this. So, Luba's parents hired another teacher who came to their home each day after school to teach Hebrew to Luba and her brothers.

Luba enjoyed learning to read and write Hebrew. But her favorite teacher who came to the house was Mikhail. Always cheerful, Mikhail gave her—just her—art lessons.

Luba had gone to school from age eight until twelve without a problem. Then the pogroms, the

Cossack raids, began. Government persecution of Jews crept more into daily life. Something awful was happening throughout the town and the entire nation. Laws against Jews limited what they could do and where they could go. To make things worse, Russia experienced some lean harvests. Starving Russian peasants raided lands in the fertile Ukraine for food. This left some villages in Ukraine to starve. For some reason, other Ukrainians also blamed the Jews for their troubles. Now several different bands of roving thugs attacked Jewish communities like the one in Zhitomir.

After the most recent Cossack raid, Luba noticed changes at school, too. A new government that had overthrown the Russian royal family now expanded into Ukraine and dictated orders for everything, including schools. The new Soviet Union, as Russia was called in 1922, limited the amount of food and goods families could buy. Leaders ordered that children learn ideas to further government-approved thinking. Children learned Communist worker songs and painted pictures of workers and soldiers that taught the philosophy of the Soviet Union.

Communists believed that religion was the root of all evil. So, Luba's teachers began teaching that all religions were bad. They told the students that wealthy people who owned land and factories were bad. Worst of all, the Communist government leaders and teachers taught that war and hate against anyone who disagreed with them was a good thing.

Now teachers felt they could let their hate for certain groups, mainly Jews, show. Luba's classmates who had heard nasty things about Jews from their parents started spreading lies about the Jewish girls at school. Both teachers and other students shamed Jewish girls by making mean, anti-Jewish statements. They called Luba and her Jewish friends names. They taunted Luba on her way to school and on the way home. She no longer had any friends who were not Jewish.

At first, the insults against Luba were mild. Then the sickness against Jews grew worse. Finally, Luba's teacher told her parents to keep her home from school. She was no longer welcome, no matter how well she did with her studies.

4

Papa Turns Purple

About a week after Luba was forced to leave school, a letter came for Papa. The letter ordered Papa to report to a government office to become a Russian soldier. Papa paced the floor trying to figure out what to do. He and Mama knew how terrible the army would be for Papa and the family. He would be harassed or punished or worse for being Jewish. Without Papa's income, Mama would have to find work, which was nearly impossible, or beg to keep the family afloat.

"How can I leave my family and go into the army?" he asked Mama. "You would have to fend for yourselves without money. And I don't agree with our government. They oppose religion of any kind. They hate our Jewish religion most of all. They punish anyone with different ideas. I would never last."

Mama and Papa talked about what to do. "It is time to write to your brother in Chicago," Mama said. "Maybe he can help us go to America."

Papa agreed to write to Luba's Uncle Velvel that night. In the meantime, Papa wanted to talk with his friends. He left the house and found many men at the market who had received the same letter as he did. No one could think of how to get out of serving a government they couldn't stand.

On his way home, Papa stopped by the drugstore of his friend, Boris. Papa told Boris what was happening. They talked about how awful the government was. Papa shared with Boris his fears about being away from his family.

As Papa was leaving, Boris called him back. "I just thought of something that might help you get out of the army, my friend," he said. "I have a powder that changes skin color to a purple look of death. You will seem ill and unfit for the army. But your usual color and spirit will return with time. That's a promise."

Boris handed Papa a small white sack. "Empty the powder into a half glass of water the night before you report to the army. Drink it slowly. In a few hours, you will see a difference. Don't be frightened. Maybe your look will help change the officer's mind about taking you into the army."

When Papa returned home, he talked with Mama about what he should do. Mama trusted Boris. "I will do as you and Boris say," Papa decided. "First, I will write to my brother in America."

The day before his tests for the army, Papa prayed. Then he drank Boris's powder in water. That night, Papa was so upset about the drink and the army that he hardly slept.

The next morning Luba looked at her father in horror. "Papa, you look awful!" she cried. "You're purple! Are you sick?"

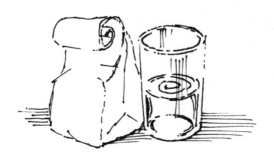

Papa checked his face in the mirror. Sure enough, he looked terrible from lack of sleep. But his purple face and body made him look even sicker. Fayvish cried. Mama hugged the little children.

Papa tried to calm them with words he remembered from Boris. "I'll be fine. That's a promise," he said. "Hopefully, being purple will let me come home to you, rather than join the horrible army."

At the army office, men moved away from Papa as he walked past them. No one had ever seen someone who looked like a walking dead man. Two soldiers ran to Papa's side and led him to the officer's desk. He asked Papa some questions. Then the officer ordered Papa to go home. "Tell your wife to take you to the hospital—at once," he said.

Papa could not believe his fortune. Neither could Mama and the children when they heard what had happened. Luba hugged her purple father. Mama cried from joy. Everyone knew there was still danger for them in Zhitomir. But for now, the family was safe.

Time to Leave

1923

Papa kept writing to his brother in Chicago. One time Uncle Velvel answered that money was tight for him. He would have trouble finding enough to bring the entire family to America by ship. Could Papa offer any help?

Papa barely made enough now to feed his family. Without his shop, he had to find odd jobs. He sang prayers in temple. He sewed shoes for others. He patched wagon seats. He built furniture. But he received little pay. He could never save enough for so many ship tickets.

Another time Luba's uncle wrote that new laws only allowed a certain number of people from each country into the United States. And the law required Papa to have a job before the family could enter. Uncle Velvel promised to work as fast as he could, but making plans would take time. Papa needed to be patient.

But how could they be patient when the food cupboards looked so bare? Other families had already gotten sick from lack of food. Mama worried they would be next. Papa kept sending letters to Uncle Velvel, describing how hopeless their life had become. In private, Papa and Mama wondered if solving their problems was beyond hope.

During fall of 1923, Uncle Velvel sent Papa another letter. Velvel wanted to know the names and birthdates of each person in the family. He needed the information quickly.

Papa wrote him back at once. "I have a strange feeling about Velvel. Perhaps he found a way to bring us to America," he told Mama as he wrote. "Could our prayers finally be answered?"

"Be sure to tell Velvel that you have been

cantor at temple, singing and leading services," Mama said. "Maybe, just maybe, a temple in Chicago could use your talent."

Papa did as Mama suggested. He also thanked his brother for helping. He promised to repay any costs.

For weeks, the Dichnes heard nothing. Then one day toward the end of 1923, another letter arrived from Uncle Velvel. As Papa opened the letter, seven tickets for the ship, SS *Estonia*, dropped out.

"Look children. Come quickly," Papa shouted. "We're going to America."

Papa hugged Mama and the children. Luba grabbed Sonia and spun her around in circles. The family danced the hora—and without music. Their joy was music enough.

The days ahead were busy. Luba went with Papa to the government office to ask permission for them to leave. Luckily, Russia was thrilled to be rid of seven Jews.

Once they had permission, the family prepared to travel to Riga, Latvia, to get proper papers and a checkup. After their checkup, they must take a train to another Latvia town, Libawa, to wait for the ship.

A jumble of thoughts spun through Luba's mind. She was excited to be leaving a place where her family was not wanted. In America they could practice their religion whenever and wherever they wanted. They would be safe. She could go to school.

But she was leaving the only home she had ever known. She would miss her house and friends and neighbors. Most of all, she would miss her grandparents and Mikhail, her kind-hearted art teacher. And then there was the difficult job of packing.

"Each of you can take just one suitcase," Papa said. "That's all we have room for."

Luba hated packing. How could she choose what to take? Most of all, she hated parting with her toys. Mama said she had to leave her favorite life-sized doll behind.

"She's much too big to bring on a train and boat," Mama said when Luba asked to keep the doll. "And we have no idea how much room we will have in our new home in Chicago."

"But she opens and closes her eyes," Luba cried.

"I promise to buy you a new doll in America," Mama said, putting her arm around Luba. "But you can take your painted pin with a gold chain that Grandpa gave you. It will remind you of people and places you loved in Ukraine."

Luba looked around the dining room. "What about my pictures?" she asked.

"Why don't you let your grandfather, grandmother, and Mikhail choose their favorites. That way, they will have something from you to remember," Mama suggested.

Mama looked Luba in the eye. "Soon you will be thirteen, Luba," Mama continued. "You are almost grown up. Moving is part of life." Luba tried to understand.

Mama and Papa went through their things, too. They needed to decide what to give away, what to throw out, and what to bring. In the end, they took just enough household tools, linens, and kitchen supplies to get them started in their new home. Of course, they packed the Shabbat candles. In America, they could light Friday night candles and keep the holy day of Sabbath again. No more secret prayers, as they were forced to say in hiding.

Mama told everyone to wear layers of light clothes. This saved room in their suitcases for other clothes. To keep warm, they wore fur-lined coats that they would carry, not pack.

Mama and Papa worried that the guards who searched them would take their money. So they each carried just enough money for the trip. Luba and Mama sewed the rest of their savings into the hems of their winter coats.

Before leaving, Mikhail visited Luba one last time. He gave her a slate pencil, colored pencils, and blank notebook. This was her goodbye present. "Draw me the biggest, brightest picture of

America, my little artist," he told her. He hugged her tightly. After Mikhail left, Luba made sure to find room for his gift in her suitcase.

Once everyone had filled their suitcases, it was time to say goodbye. Family and friends gathered at their house one last time. Men kissed men. Women kissed women. This Russian custom usually made everyone happy. Yet it was a sad custom today.

Luba found leaving her grandparents and dear art teacher the hardest of all. She had no idea when or if she'd ever see them again. She would never forget any of them. Tears filled her eyes as everyone waved good-bye.

Papa hired a driver with horses and a wagon to take them to the train. At the station, each Dichne carried a suitcase onto the train. "Why are there no seats?" Luba asked Papa.

"Our journey is short, Luba. Sit on your suitcase," Papa said.

Sure enough, the train ride ended only an hour later. Once in Libawa, men directed the Dichne family to a special space in a large room. There they waited with other travelers for the ship to arrive.

After dark, Luba quickly fell asleep on a mat on the floor of the big room. The train ride and excitement of going somewhere new had tired her. She dreamed of America.

6

Twin Trouble

Early the next morning, Sonia shook Luba awake. "I don't feel well," she said.

Luba saw her red face and woke Mama. Mama touched Sonia's forehead. "She's burning up," she cried.

Mama made a warm bed for Sonia at the station. Mama couldn't imagine the illness lasting very long, so they decided to stay near the boat dock. Meanwhile, Mama pressed cold cloths on Sonia's head.

Each day, Sonia felt a little cooler. But the fever lasted for a week before the little five-year-old was up and acting like herself again.

By the time Sonia felt better, Yankel caught her fever. Now it was Luba's littlest brother's turn to lay in bed and have cold cloths on his head. Like his twin sister, he barely moved. He ate little.

While the twins grew stronger, the *Estonia* came and went. The family would have to stay in Libawa until the ship returned. Waiting was hard, but at least they were still going to America. Luba used the time to draw pictures in her new notebook.

Finally, the *Estonia* returned. Luba clapped her hands and jumped up and down at the sight of the huge boat pulling up to the dock. The three-chimney ship had eight decks, one on top of the other.

"Papa, I've never seen anything so long and tall," Luba said.

Once the ship anchored, the call came to board. Each member of the Dichne family carried their own suitcase. Luba struggled to get hers up the steep stairs leading to the deck of the ship. But friendly sailors greeted them and offered to help. One man took Luba's suitcase and led her to the room where she and Sonia would sleep.

Luba and her family followed the man down several staircases to the bottom three decks of the ship. These decks contained cabins for passengers. The bottom deck was where the poorer people slept. On the lowest deck, at the bottom of the ship, the seven Dichnes shared a row of tiny cabins.

Luba and Sonia went in the first cabin. "Oh," Luba exclaimed. "This cabin feels smaller than my wardrobe at home."

The boys went into the cabin next to Luba's. Mama and Papa put their suitcases and bags in the cabin on the other side of the boys. The cabins were snug, but no one else complained. They were together, and they were going to America.

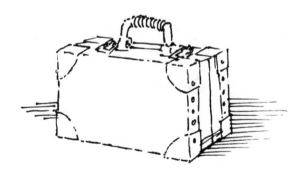

PICTURE GIRL

7

Bad Dreams

"Mama, Mama, please help me!" Fayvish shouted over and over.

Her brother's screams jolted Luba awake. Even through the cabin wall, she recognized her brother's sharp cries. Luba hated when her brother sounded like he'd seen a monster. His nightmares took her back to their neighbor's cramped cellar. Once again, Luba was afraid of her shadow. Afraid of any sounds. Afraid to move.

The third-class deck where they slept lay below the water line. No sunlight or moonlight shined into Luba's room. Noisy waves lapped against the side of the boat. With the candle out, the cabin seemed dark and scary.

Luba slid down to the foot of the ship's bunk. She pulled the cover tightly over her head. More pictures of the Warshaver's damp, dark cellar flashed through her mind. She remembered how the Cossacks had caused fear everywhere in town. Would the bandits steal their few things? Would they kill them as they had others in Zhitomir—just because they were Jewish?

Luba poked a finger into each ear to block Fayvish's sobs. Then she heard Mama in Fayvish's cabin. "Mama's here, little one. You just had a bad dream."

Mama's gentle voice floated through the thin walls. "Remember we are on a boat," she said. "A boat to America. No one can hurt us now."

Luba had hoped Fayvish's bad dreams would go away once they were at sea. Yet, each night his nightmares returned, reminding Luba of those awful Cossacks. But she tried to calm herself with thoughts of America.

Tonight, she imagined Uncle Velvel's home in Chicago, where they were headed. She pictured tree-lined streets and tall grasses where her Papa's brother lived. She saw blue, yellow, and purple flowers, just like home in Zhitomir. Luba imagined her new school. Unlike back home, the American school would never expel her for being Jewish.

Mikhail, her Ukrainian art teacher, appeared in her imagination, too. She grinned at the thought of his pointy chin, big eyes, and wide smile. How she loved to paint with this kind, giving man. He painted pictures with watercolors and gave them to Luba. He let her practice with his paints. Her job was to copy the pictures, colors and all. From these lessons, she learned to mix paints into different colors. He taught her how to draw people, scenes, and designs.

In her imagination, Luba watched her gifted hands fly over the paper in the notebook Mikhail had given her. She drew faces like those in photos her uncle had sent. With each dream drawing, Fayvish and the Cossacks faded further away. Luba drifted deeper into sleep.

PICTURE GIRL

8

The Terrible Storm

The next morning began the same as the three before. Luba and Sonia awoke, and Luba helped Sonia wash in the cabin's tiny sink. Then the two knocked on their parents' door. Soon the three boys joined them in their parent's room. Together the family started up the stairs to the second deck for breakfast in the dining room.

Luba followed Sonia up the long flight of stairs. About halfway up, the boat began to bump and roll. Luba grabbed the railing with one hand and Sonia with the other. She held tightly to keep them from slamming into the narrow stairway.

Slowly, Luba pushed Sonia onto the open deck.

"The ship must have hit a big wave," Luba yelled to Sonia above the ocean's roar. Luba's heart beat wildly, but she tried to sound brave for her little sister. "The rocking will soon pass."

But the rocking only grew worse. The boat tossed out of control in the foamy waves. Water splashed over the side, making the girls slip on the wet deck. Dark gray clouds like those Luba painted in her most angry pictures swirled overhead. Wind whipped through the smokestacks. Everything that was not tied down slid from side to side, including people. Luba clung to a post to keep them from falling.

The crashing waves reminded Luba of Cossacks smashing down doors. Screams came from all around her, just like at home. Luba bit her lip not to cry. What if the boat breaks apart? Please don't let us die at sea, she prayed.

"Come children. Let's return to our cabins," Papa called out over the roar of the sea.

Luba took Sonia's shaky hand and started down the stairs. As they followed the rest of her family, Fayvish tripped. He tumbled to the bottom of the stairway and landed with a thud. His head banged the corner of the hard bottom stair. Blood spilled from the wound, covering his face. Papa rushed to help him.

"Oh no," Luba cried. She stopped on the stairs and held her breath. She squeezed Sonia's hand to keep her still.

Just then, the captain's order came over the loudspeaker: "Please go to your cabins and put on life jackets."

Mama called out for a doctor. But everyone was too busy with the storm to help her find one. People hurried around them, trying to reach their cabins. Many held one hand over their mouth to keep down the seasickness.

Little by little, the walkways cleared. The ship's doctor appeared to check families in their cabins. As he looked down the hall, he spotted Fayvish crying in Papa's bloody lap. The doctor bent over him and wiped away the blood. He covered Fayvish's head with a clean cloth.

Fayvish seemed well enough to walk. Still, Papa carried him to his cabin. Luba, her brothers, sister, and Mama stumbled after them. The boat rolled them one way then another. Luba's stomach rose into her throat. She couldn't wait to find her bed.

"The storm is very bad," the captain shouted again over the loudspeaker. "It comes at us from everywhere. The only place to go is back the way we came. For how long, we can't tell. It's our only hope. Thank you for staying calm."

For four days that seemed like weeks, the ship bobbed and bumped on the rolling sea. Rain pelted the decks, keeping everyone in their cabins. Luba ate little. Usually, she liked to copy pictures she found in books to pass the time. But she felt too weak. Instead, she sucked a lump of salt to help her hold down the bigger lump in her throat. And she prayed they would live to see America.

On the fifth morning, Luba awoke to quiet. The rocking had stopped. The sea gently lapped at the side of the boat. The storm had ended.

"We're safe," Papa said. He hugged Luba as she entered his cabin. "The captain turned the ship around at daybreak. We're heading for America again."

Luba raced onto the open deck and took a

deep breath of fresh, salty air. She bathed her face in warm sun from the cloudless sky. Wind tossed her long blond hair. Luba delighted in the glassy water that shone in her favorite deep-green color. I must draw this day, she decided.

Luba returned to the cabin to find her pencils and notebook. She carried them back to the open deck, then plopped into a slatted wooden chair and thought about what to draw. And she let herself dream of America once again.

9

Lady with a Torch

After 18 days on the ocean, the SS *Estonia* sailed into New York harbor. The Dichne family dragged their suitcases up the stairs and onto the deck. Crowds of shouting, waving people lined the railing. Luba and her family squeezed toward the front of the ship. Everyone wanted to see America.

Slowly, the boat crept toward the port of Manhattan in New York City. Here is where the family would receive permission to enter the United States. Then Luba's family could catch the train to Chicago.

Tall skyscrapers stood like soldiers on the right. Rocks lined the shore. To the left, a large statue towered over the boat. Its gray concrete and brick base held a giant copper woman.

"Who is that big green lady? And why does her right arm hold up something that glows in the sun?" Luba asked her father.

"Uncle Velvel wrote to me about her, Luba, my little one," Papa said. He put his arm around Luba and leaned closer to talk in her ear. "She is the Statue of Liberty. Uncle Velvel says she is here to welcome us. She holds a gold torch to light our way. She gives us hope that our dreams to live in peace will come true."

"I like this lady," Luba said. "I will try to remember what she looks like. I want to draw her picture later."

Papa smiled. "I think that's a wonderful idea," he said.

The closer the boat got to the port the larger the buildings became. Low gray dots on the island turned into huge skyscrapers. Waiting taxis formed a line at the end of the pier.

While they talked, Luba noticed some people from the *Estonia* filing off the boat. Seeing them move, Luba grabbed her suitcase, too.

"Not yet, Luba," Papa said. "We must wait for the rich people from the decks above us to get off first."

Luba's round cheeks turned red. She stamped her foot. "That's not fair, Papa," she objected. "We were supposed to be here in 8 days. We were at sea for 18. How could we be so close to America now and not be allowed off the boat?"

Mama shot Luba one of her looks. "Hush!" Mama whispered sharply. "Don't make trouble.'

Luba bit her lip to keep quiet. She knew better than to say more. Mama would never allow it. So she frowned at the people in fine clothes leaving the boat. Many hired men on the dock just to carry their bags. Some went straight into waiting taxis.

What makes them so special? Luba wondered. This is America. This is where everyone is supposed to be equal.

Luba's family waited for almost half an hour to leave. Finally, it was their turn. Luba followed her sister and brothers off the boat. But they weren't allowed to go into the city. Guards told them to board a ferry to nearby Ellis Island.

"Why can't we go yet?" Luba asked Mama.

"Soon enough, soon enough," Mama said. She put her hand on Luba's shoulder. She tried to calm Luba and herself.

10

Entering Ellis Island

Too many people crowded into the tiny boat. Grownups shoved. Babies cried. Luba squeezed into a seat between Sonia and Moysey. She felt tired from the trip, tired of waiting, and tired of being pushed. Yet she squirmed and jiggled in her seat.

"Stop jumping around," Moysey whined. He poked her to stop.

"I can't believe we're almost in America!" she told him with a broad grin.

The boat pulled next to the Ellis Island dock.

Luba counted 34 different red brick and plaster buildings. The ship dropped anchor near the biggest one. Four pointy stations with guards stood in each corner of the building. A flag waved in front. It had red and white stripes and white stars on a blue background.

Luba helped Sonia off the boat. Each child dragged their suitcase containing only a few articles of clothing. But each piece of clothing was important because of the gold coins sewn into the hems of pants and skirts. Once in America, they planned to trade the coins for American money.

The Dichnes followed other families from the boat. They marched down a walkway into the main building. Luba lugged her bag upstairs and into a large room on the second floor. Her soft blue eyes opened wide as they entered the room.

"I've never seen such a big room," she whispered to Moysey. "It's much bigger and fancier than the Libawa train station."

A high ceiling made of smooth brick arched over the room. Three round-topped windows lit each side of the huge hall. Another window let in light at the ends of the room. Tile went halfway up the walls. This made the room noisy with all the jabbering, excited people. Guards watched from a third-floor open walkway. From that height, they could see everyone in the hall.

Luba tugged on Papa's coat sleeve. "Look at those guards. They have sticks," she whispered.

"Quiet, my little Luba. All will be well," he promised.

Long benches stretched as far as Luba could see. They formed rows for standing and sitting. Railings kept the newcomers divided in lines. A man sat behind a desk at the end of each row. His job was to check the bags and papers of each person before they could enter the United States. He counted the number of people from a given country. If there were too many, the extras were sent back to where they started, just like Uncle Velvel had written in his letter.

Luba knew America already had enough people from the Ukraine for 1923. But Papa was special. He could sing. He sang beautiful Russian and Yiddish folk songs to her often. Mama's idea to remind Uncle Velvel of his brother's talent had proved just the thing to get them to America. Luba's uncle had found Papa a job as cantor to sing at a Chicago temple. There was no chance they would be sent home. Or could they?

11

Unexpected Stay

The Dichnes waited in line for about an hour. When it was their turn, Papa spoke for the family. He opened their bags to be inspected. He gave the man their papers and pointed to each family member. But Papa only spoke Russian and Yiddish. He couldn't understand what the man was asking.

Another man who spoke Yiddish came to help the two men talk to each other. Just then, the first man saw Fayvish's covered head and pulled him out of line. He said some words no one understood. This brought a guard who was standing nearby. The guard pulled Fayvish toward the door.

"Where are you taking him?" Papa yelled in Yiddish. Mama and Fayvish started to cry. Luba drew Sonia and Yankel closer to protect them. The guards looked like soldiers from home.

Why are they taking Fayvish from us? Luba worried. Could guards act the same in America as in Ukraine? She would take care of Fayvish, as she always had. He wouldn't cause any trouble. Luba dug her fingernails into her hand to fight back the tears welling up in her eyes.

"Please understand," the second man told Papa in Yiddish. "Your son is not in trouble. His wound looks bad. He needs to see a doctor. Your family can wait on Ellis Island until he is out of the hospital."

"No!" Papa shouted, looking beaten. "The twins were sick and we missed our first boat. The boat we took hit a storm and turned back. Now this." Before Papa could say more, the second man led him toward the doorway. The rest of the family gathered their bags and followed.

What will become of Fayvish? Luba worried. What will become of us?

12

More Lines

The man told Papa and the boys to stand in one line with other men. He showed Mama and the girls where they should wait with the other women. "You will all be in America soon enough," he said. "For now, you must follow the rules while your son gets better."

The Dichnes stood in one line after another. Each line led to a different doctor. One woman checked Luba's eyes, nose, and ears. Someone else looked into her mouth. Another doctor pounded on her chest. The same doctor tapped a little hammer on her knees and tickled her back.

"Why do they do these things?" Luba asked Mama. "I'm not sick."

"They want to make sure we are well and strong enough to work in America," Mama said.

"Hurry up! Push, push, push! These Americans treat us like cattle at the market," Luba whispered.

"At least we are in America," Mama said, trying to hush her.

Luba looked around to pass the time in line. "Why do doctors put an *X* on some people's backs?" she asked.

"I'm not sure. But look how those people are told to step aside," Mama answered. "Maybe they have something wrong with them. That woman just turned her coat inside out. I'll bet she is trying to trick the guards by not showing her *X*."

Luba looked at Mama while they talked. She noticed how straight and tall Mama stood. That's a sign we're safe now, she thought. Before, Mama's fear and sadness made her body sag. The long boat ride, even the storm, was worth the trouble, she decided.

Every so often, Luba ran her hand along the hem of her coat. She checked that the gold coins were safe. They needed the money to travel to Chicago and live there. They had to pay Uncle Velvel back for the boat tickets.

Finally, the string of lines ended. Luba and her sister and mother returned to the big, noisy room. "We passed our tests," Luba shouted to Papa and the boys.

"So did we," said Yankel.

Luba hugged her father, Yankel, and Moysey. "Why are we in this room again?" she asked Papa.

"We must wait for someone to show us where to store our things," Papa said.

Luba's smile faded. She badly wanted to leave Ellis Island. But of course they would never go without Fayvish.

Soon a large group gathered in the big room. From the smiles on their faces, Luba knew that these people had passed their tests, too.

A guard appeared to take them on a tour of the building. They saw the dining room. They were given beds in sleeping rooms. There was one sleeping room for men and boys and one for women and girls. They learned where the business office, hospital, post office, and showers were. The children saw school rooms on the second floor and met the head teacher.

"Everyone seems nice enough," Luba told Moysey. "Perhaps this won't be too bad."

13

Living on Ellis Island

Luba was surprised at how quickly the days passed. The guards and other workers took good care of them. She and her family found many things to do.

Mama and Papa visited Fayvish every day during visiting hours in the hospital. When Papa needed a break, he went into the yard in the back of the building to exercise with the other men. Other times, the family took books to read out of a room called a library. Ukraine never had stacks of books to read for free. This library not only had free books, but its shelves included books in almost every language. Mama chose books in Russian. Luba and Papa read books in Russian and Hebrew.

Luba, Moysey, Sonia, and Yankel went to school for much of each day. The teacher taught them some English words. They danced and sang English children's songs, much like they had done in kindergarten in Ukraine. As one of the oldest children, Luba often helped with the younger ones. Luba liked taking the littlest ones to the children's backyard. Here they played on swings, a seesaw, and a merry-go-round.

Luba also learned about the U.S. flag and how to say the Pledge of Allegiance. She proudly sang the "Star Spangled Banner," America's national anthem. She vowed to be the best American she could be.

After school, families gathered in their sleeping rooms, where the beds had been folded up to make a sitting room. Luba usually took out her notebook to draw. Every day she practiced a special way she had discovered to copy pictures she found in books. She used strips of paper to enlarge the pictures. She carefully measured each feature with a paper strip two or three times as big as the original. One by one, she added a new feature to her picture. The final result was a picture much bigger than the original.

Back home, Luba had copied pictures of many famous people this way. Exact likenesses of writers, poets, and scientists covered the family living and dining room walls. Everyone who had looked at those pictures believed Luba would grow up to be an artist someday. So did Luba.

On Ellis Island, Luba taught Moysey how to copy pictures in this special way. She gave paper to the other children, too. That way, she could draw and help watch them at the same time. Drawing together proved helpful because, at thirteen years of age, she was expected to help in the family like a grownup.

Each night, Luba slept with 35 other women and girls in a room on the third floor. Luba, Mama, and Sonia lay one above the other in three heavy cloth bunk beds. Bars covered the windows of the room, and three sinks lined one wall. Papa and the boys slept in a similar room on the other side of the floor.

Luba and her family ate three meals a day at

tables as long as the huge tiled dining room. Other chattering families sat on both sides of each table. They passed large platters of food that workers on the island had prepared for them.

Luba had never seen so many different people in such a big restaurant. Many of them had skin that was a different color from hers and wore strange, colorful costumes. Luba had studied about dark-skinned people in her Ukrainian school. But she had never actually met anyone like the people she saw on Ellis Island. Mama had taught her not to stare. Still, she couldn't take her eyes off one cute little girl with dark brown skin and short, tight, curly braids.

Some of the meals they were served were new to Luba, too. The stews, pudding, pickled herring, and boiled beef reminded Luba of home. More often, though, she ate American food like chicken, ice cream, and white bread. Unlike Sonia, who would only eat food she recognized, Luba tried everything. She believed eating these foods would help make her a good American.

One day, Luba found a long, thin object on

her lunch plate. "How do you eat such a thing?" she asked Moysey. He shrugged.

Luba shyly poked at the firm yellow skin like it was alive. Nothing happened. Then she noticed a man at the other end of the table peeling the skin. Luba watched him bite a chunk of its soft white insides.

"Now I know what to do with this strange food," Luba said, gently breaking the skin.

"I think it's a fruit called *banana*," Mama said, bending toward her. Mama told her the word more slowly in English. Luba repeated the word and took a bite.

"So sweet," Luba said. "I want more of these when we get to Chicago."

14

More Bad News

After two weeks, the doctor finally released Fayvish from the hospital. Luba hardly recognized him. His head was shaved. His nearly-hairless skin showed a row of pink lines where the doctor had sewn the cut closed. Luba realized how serious his fall really had been.

"How strange Fayvish looks," she whispered to Moysey. Mama and Papa paid no attention to how Fayvish looked. They just smiled broad smiles and hugged him.

Fayvish let each of them touch his fuzzy head. As Luba took her turn, she noticed a guard calling

Mama and Papa aside. He walked them toward the office, which she took as a bad sign. The guards here had proven to be very kind. Still, her heart beat faster whenever one appeared. She didn't say a word to her brothers and sister, who didn't seem to notice. But she worried about why her parents were taken away.

When Mama and Papa came out of the office, their smiles had disappeared. Mama sagged into a seat and buried her face in her hands. Her shoulders shook as she softly cried. Papa lowered himself beside her. He hung his head down, refusing to look at anyone.

After a few minutes, Luba could stand the sadness no longer. "What's the matter?" she asked.

Papa looked up at her. Then he gathered the children around him. As he spoke, Luba could hardly hear his words.

"We are too late," he said slowly. "Other people took our place to stay in America. We have to go back to Ukraine when our ship returns."

"Oh no!" Luba cried, not believing what she heard. "What about the special list you were on, Papa?"

"Even that special list is now full," Papa said sadly. "They want no more people from Ukraine in the United States."

Luba's eyes flashed with anger. "That's not fair! We did nothing wrong. What will become of us?"

"Life is not always fair," Mama said wiping the tears from her eyes. She sat up and took a deep breath, trying to look strong. "With God's help, we will make do somehow."

Mama talked bravely. But Luba saw the pain in her eyes. We can't go home, Luba thought. Jews are not welcome in Ukraine. Papa would go to jail. None of us could find work. We could be killed. I must think of some way to keep us in America.

"Now I know why some people call Ellis Island the 'Isle of Tears,'" Luba said. "So many people like us cry when the United States turns us away."

In the days that followed, Mama and Papa talked about their problems with other families in the big room. Luba mostly kept to herself. Drawing pictures was the only thing that made her feel better. Drawing helped her think.

"Why don't you play with your sister and brothers?" Mama begged her. But Luba stayed by herself.

"What can we possibly do with all these pictures?" Mama asked. "We have no room for them in our bags." Still, Luba continued to draw.

One day, Luba looked up from her picture and noticed something strange about Sonia. She put down her picture and dragged Sonia over to Mama.

"Mama," Luba called. "Look at Sonia's red bumps."

Mama studied Sonia's face closely. Then she pulled Sonia's blouse out and checked her chest and back.

"Oh dear. She must have measles," Mama cried. She called the guard and pointed to Sonia's face. The guard took Sonia's hand and led her and Mama to the doctor's office. Sure enough, the doctor said, Mama was right. Sonia had measles. And others could easily catch the sickness. Sonia needed to be away from other people and in the hospital until all her spots disappeared.

Sonia stayed in the hospital for ten days. During that time, the *Estonia* came and went.

"We will board the ship when it returns again," Papa said with a sigh.

But by the time Sonia left the hospital, Yankel had caught the measles. Again, the family waited for someone in the hospital. Again, the ship came and went.

"This gives me time to think of a plan. I so want to help my family stay here," Luba thought many times.

15

Luba Keeps Drawing

During her long stay on Ellis Island, Luba made many friends. A few of them gave her pictures of their family from home to draw. There was so little to do, her friends often watched her work.

One day, a woman handed Luba a picture of U. S. President Woodrow Wilson. He had just died, and his picture was in the newspaper. Luba placed the picture on the floor in front of her. She picked up a pencil and carefully made lines. She checked how long and wide each marking should be with strips of paper. First, Luba formed a round head. Then she added eyes and Wilson's bushy eyebrows and fixed mouth. One by one, the features turned into an exact likeness of the president.

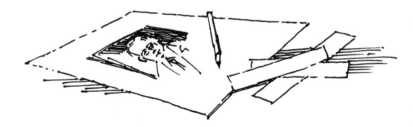

A crowd gathered as Luba drew. The guards assumed that large groups of people meant trouble. A pot-bellied guard pushed his way toward Luba. As he pushed closer, the onlookers scattered. The guard looked surprised to find Luba sitting in the center of the crowd. Several pencil drawings of President Wilson were spread on the floor around her.

"Who drew these pictures?" he asked picking up a drawing. Someone who spoke English pointed to Luba. The guard shook his head.

"Such a young girl to draw so well," he said. Then a smile spread across his face.

"Come with me," he ordered Luba. He collected the pictures and pointed toward the door.

As Luba stood, her legs wobbled like a baby learning to walk. What did I do wrong? she wondered. What will the guard do to me? She noticed her parents from across the room. Their frightened looks made Luba worry even more.

The guard took Luba into an office near the schoolroom. Three other men joined them. The guard talked quickly in English. Luba hardly understood a word. The men listened, looked at the pictures, and then turned to Luba.

One man pointed to a chair. After Luba sat down, he handed her some pencils, erasers, and paper. Another man took a picture of President George Washington off the wall. He carefully laid it on the table in front of Luba.

These men don't believe I can draw, Luba thought. They want to watch me copy the picture from the wall. I'll show them.

Luba always liked to draw for others. But these guards made her feel funny. She squirmed in her seat. Her body grew hot. The men watched and quietly waited for her to begin. Luba just stared at the paper.

After a few minutes, she forced herself to pick up a pencil. She placed it on the paper, not sure where to begin. Once she started drawing, however, she forgot the guards standing over her.

After she finished, Luba looked up. All four men stood smiling. One asked to take the picture to show someone. Luba shook her head. She just wanted to leave. The drawing had taken almost an hour. Mama and Papa would be worried.

The guard took Luba back to the room with the others. As she entered the room, she saw her parent's faces brighten.

"Where have you been for so long, little one?" Mama asked hugging her. "We have been beside ourselves with worry."

Luba told them about the guards and the drawing. "At least no one was harmed," Papa said, still worried about the guards. "You must be very careful until the boat comes. Watch that your pictures do not get you into trouble."

16

Letters to Uncle Velvel

Later that day, Mama suggested that Papa write another letter to Uncle Velvel. Papa had already sent two letters since they arrived. Both said they would be late but still coming to Chicago.

"Tell him we have to go back," Mama suggested. "Thank him for what he has done."

Papa wrote about how they had lived on Ellis Island for almost three months. He explained about the storm, Fayvish's fall, and each twin's illnesses. He thanked his brother but said that, sadly, they could not stay in the United States. At the close of the letter, Papa told the story of the guard and

Luba's picture of George Washington. He said that Moysey was talented, too. He knew his children could make a future for themselves in America. "But now that seems out of the question," Papa ended the letter.

Within a week, Papa received a letter from Uncle Velvel. He asked if Papa could mail him some of Luba's drawings.

"What a nice thank you gift for my brother," Papa agreed. He rolled and wrapped Luba's pictures along with some made by Moysey. He took them to the Ellis Island post office for mailing. Ten days later, the *Estonia* pulled into the port.

"As soon as the boat is clean we leave," Luba grumbled to Moysey, their noses pressed against the window. "But I want to stay here. I want to draw pictures of America forever."

After two days, the boat was ready to board. A guard appeared in the big room with a pile of yellow and pink papers. Families who received a yellow paper had to leave the United States. Pink papers meant they could stay in the country.

Everyone but the Dichnes crowded around the guard to hear better. Luba's family waited in the back of the room. They knew what was in store for them—a yellow paper and a long boat ride to Ukraine.

PICTURE GIRL

17

Surprise News

First, the guard called off the names of those who were to leave. One by one, those families lined up at the door. But the Dichnes never heard their name. Papa thought there must be a mix-up.

Then the guard read the list of names to receive pink slips. At the top of the list was the Dichne family!

Mama and Papa hugged. Tears rolled down their faces. Luba pinched her arm to make sure she wasn't dreaming. Everyone in the family was too stunned to come forward for their pink paper.

The guard called their name again, this time louder. "The Dichne family for America," he sang with a smile. "Start packing!"

"You heard the man," Papa ordered with a grin. Mama worried it was all a mistake. Luba didn't care if it was. She wanted to be an American more than anything. She pushed Sonia and Yankel toward their bags.

Luba and her family boarded a ferry for Manhattan. Uncle Velvel had sent someone to meet them at the pier. The woman spoke Yiddish. She knew how to get them to Uncle Velvel. First, she took them to a building with many floors of people. They were to stay there until their train left for Chicago. The whole time, Luba and her parents wondered what had changed their luck.

As the woman rose to leave, Papa could stand it no longer. "Can you tell us how we got to stay in America?" he asked.

"Thank the picture girl," the woman said, looking at Luba. "Her uncle loved the pictures you sent. He hired a lawyer to go to Washington and argue your case before a judge. The judge learned that you had a job, sir. But he also knew that your children showed great talent, especially Luba. He decided that no one in your family would ever go hungry with a girl who could draw such wonderful pictures."

Luba beamed with pride. Yes, she thought, I *am* the picture girl. An American picture girl.

Afterword

Two days later, the Dichnes arrived in Chicago. Uncle Velvel, who now called himself William Dunn, met them at the train. Papa presented Mama and each of the children to William. When he got to Luba and Moysey, Uncle William gave them each an extra hug.

The story of Luba and her drawings reached a newspaper reporter. He took a photograph of Luba and Moysey pointing to their pictures on a wall. The *Chicago Herald Examiner* printed the snapshot with the headline: "Baby Artists Win Way Past (Government Immigrant) Ban." Luba and her pictures were famous in America.

Once in Chicago, the Dichne family changed its name to Dunn, too. Luba took the American name Louise. She quickly picked up more English to fit into her new country. Louise became an American girl.

But she never stopped drawing. In high school, she won an award to study at the famous School of the Art Institute of Chicago. She continued to study there through college.

After graduating from college, she painted pictures and made prints that she sold or entered in art exhibits. She even created another new way of producing pictures. She rolled ink over a piece of glass or aluminum foil. Then she laid a piece of paper over the ink. Once the ink dried, Louise searched for lines that could be turned into scenes, objects, or designs.

Louise taught art in the Chicago Public Schools. Later, she helped teachers teach art to their students. True to her word, she grew up to be an American artist.

But Louise never forgot that her art training began with Mikhail in Ukraine. She remembered how drawing eased the pain of being left out because she was Jewish. She understood how pictures helped her meet people from other countries on Ellis Island. She knew that drawing had helped her family stay in the United States.

Now she tried to find ways for art to help other children. She wrote several books and painted pictures that showed art as a way to build good will among people. Above all else, she wanted people to get along, no matter what their race or religion.

*Louise at age one with her parents
in Zhitomir, Ukraine*

*Louise at age 13 with one of the drawings
that helped her family stay in America.
Reprinted with permission.*

Louise Dunn, Chicago, IL
August 2000

Louise Dunn with the author
Chicago, IL August 2000

Glossary

cantor: person who sings religious music and leads in prayer at Jewish services

communist: someone who believes in a system in which goods and businesses are owned in common and people work as they are able and are paid what they need

Cossacks: independent soldiers paid by the Russians to keep uprisings under control and harass certain ethnic groups, especially Jews

harass: to repeatedly annoy, harm, or bully specific people

hora: from Romania or Israel, a circle dance featured in many Jewish community celebrations

peasants: people of low social standing, usually farmers, small landowners, or laborers

persecution: cruel treatment or unjust punishment of people from a different race, religion, or social group

Shabbat: Jewish holy day each week that runs from sundown on Friday evening until sundown on Saturday evening; the day is marked by prayer, a special meal, and no labor of any kind

uprising: rebellion of a group against established rules, such as defying government laws

For Discussion

1. What did you like best about *Picture Girl*? Why? Is there anything you found troubling?

2. What scenes do you remember best? Why do you think they are more memorable to you?

3. How would you describe Luba?

4. How is transportation different today from in 1923 when Luba's family made their way to Chicago?

5. If you were told to leave your home quickly and could only bring enough to fit in one small suitcase, what would you bring?

6. Did you or someone you know move recently? Why did the family move? What was the experience like? How did it compare with Luba's?

7. How would you feel if you were suddenly kicked out of school or another organization? Or if you were bullied because of the religion your family practiced or some other reason that had nothing to do with what kind of person you are?

8. What could you do if you found people were being bullied or persecuted? What actions could you take?

9. How does this story of immigration relate to immigration stories you hear today? If so, how?

10. Is religious prejudice something you think goes on today? If so, how and where? What are some things individuals can do to stop this form of bullying?

11. Are there parts of this story or characters that remind you of yourself or someone else?

12. Do you think this book focuses more on plot or character? Why?

13. What are some of the major themes you come away with after reading *Picture Girl*?

Further Reading

FOR KIDS:

ELLIS ISLAND

National Geographic Readers: Ellis Island
2016; National Geographic Children's Books

What Was Ellis Island?
Patricia Brennan Demuth
2014, Penguin

Ellis Island (Cornerstones of Freedom Series)
Melissa McDaniel
2011; Children's Press

UKRAINE

Ukraine (Enchantment of the World)
Deborah Kent
2015; Scholastic

Ukraine (Explore the Countries)
Julie Murray
2017; Big Buddy Books

IMMIGRATION

Immigration and America (Step into History)
Steven Otfinoski
2018; Scholastic

Immigration: The 20th Century
(Primary Source Readers)
Debra J. Housel
2007; Teacher Created Materials

Immigration: Starting a New Life
(Reader's Theater Plays)
2014; Teacher Created Materials

JUDAISM

Judaism: DK Eyewitness Books
2016; DK Children

Jesse's Star (fiction: era of Russian pogroms)
Ellen Schwartz
2011, Orca Young Readers

Judaism (Global Citizens: World Religions)
Katie Marsico
2017; Cherry Lake Publishing

FOR ADULTS:

Selected Books by Louise Dunn Yochim

Building Human Relationships Through Art

1954; L.M Stein, Chicago, IL

The Harvest of Freedom:

Jewish Artists in America, 1930-1980s

(Michael Weinberg, co-author)

1989; Krantz Company Publishers

The Life and Works of Artist Rubin Steinberg:

A Biography

1999; LDY Special Publications, Chicago, IL

Perceptual Growth in Creativity

1967; International Textbook Company

Role and Impact:

The Chicago Society of Artists

1979; Chicago Society of Artists, Chicago, IL

Acknowledgements

Some books take a village to create. A hearty thank you to everyone who helped Louise's story along its journey to becoming a finished book.

I appreciate the time Jeffrey Dosik, Library Technician, National Park Service, Statue of Liberty, Ellis Island, took to answer so many of my questions. Louise's son and daughter-in-law, Shirley and Jerome Yochim, gave their time, too, to meet with me and graciously answer even more questions.

And to my many author and teacher readers, who read *Picture Girl* both before and after the story's completion—Mary Monsell, Charlotte Herman, Pat Kummer, Lucy Klocksin, Rima Lockwood, Eric Kimmel, Jon Haddon, and anyone else I missed—thank you for being my guiding lights. Of course, my favorite readers were closest to home: thanks for being supportive, Alison Targ Brill and Richard Brill.

Last but in no way least, my heartfelt gratitude goes to Nancy and Michael Sayre, Golden Alley Press, for connecting with Louise's story and allowing it to go out into the wider world.

Credits

Photographs on pages 85, 86 from the family archive of Louise Dunn, used with permission

Photographs on pages 87, 88 from the collection of the author

Back cover folk art created by Garry Killian - Freepik.com

About the Author

Marlene Targ Brill is the author of over seventy award-winning books. She most enjoys writing about children and their accomplishments.

Marlene has a bachelor's degree in special education, a master's degree in early childhood education, and has worked in the education field as a teacher, consultant, and curriculum specialist. In addition to researching and writing, Marlene also loves sharing information about what it's like to be an author with classrooms and groups.

When she isn't writing, Marlene enjoys painting. Writing *Picture Girl* gave her a chance to combine both of these passions. Marlene and her husband reside near Chicago in Wilmette, Illinois.

Marlene loves to hear from her readers. Contact her at marlene.brill@goldenalleypress.com

CPSIA information can be obtained
at www.ICGtesting.com
Printed in the USA
LVHW011707140119
603847LV00005B/567/P